For Oscar and Tavo, the original Buckaroos,
with special thanks to R. G. G. ~ S. T.

For Rachel, my little sister. ~ T. K.

tiger tales
5 River Road, Suite 128,
Wilton, CT 06897
Published in the United States 2016
Originally published in Great Britain 2016
by Little Tiger Press
Text copyright © 2016 Shanda Trent
Illustrations copyright © 2016 Tom Knight
ISBN-13: 978-1-68010-008-2
ISBN-10: 1-68010-008-4
Printed in China
LTP/1400/1247/0915
For more insight and activities,
visit us at www.tigertalesbooks.com

GiDDY-UP BUCKaRooS!

by Shanda Trent

Illustrated by
Tom Knight

tiger tales

Giddy-up, Buckaroos!
Here comes the sun.

Let's sneak past the sheriff
and round up some fun.

Grab something tasty, uno, dos, tres.

No time to clean up.
Gotta scram from this place.

Dash past
the **lobo**

that lives
in his den.

¡Ándale!
Hurry!
We fooled him again!

A stagecoach! Surround it.
Let's holler and hoot.

Now head for the hills
with this sack
full of loot.

Whoa! It's a rodeo!
Lasso this cow.

Yippee! We caught her.

¡Caramba!
Meow!

Race 'round these barrels
in cloverleaf loops.

Try not to tip them.
¡Qué lástima!
Oops.

The sheriff! She'll catch us.

Phew.

That was close.

¡Qué bueno!
We lost her.

Giddy-up!
¡Adiós!

Out in the desert.
No **agua** in sight.
Is there nothing
to quench us?

Here's something
that might!

Plip-plop
goes the rain.
Squish-squash
goes the mud.

The río is rising.
Oh, no! A flash flood!

Rescue that lizard.
We flooded his nest.

Buckaroo heroes,
the best in the West!

Shucks!
It's the sheriff.
No, don't wash
my shirt!

Vaqueros take days to
collect all this dirt.

Our bellies are grumbling
for something to eat.

Follow your nose to
the smell of mesquite.

Roast armadillo.

Yum!
Rattlesnake stew.

BREEZY
BEANS

Here, give our **amigo** a bite of it, too.

Listen! What's that?
The sheriff is near!

She'll sneak up
and brand us.

¡Venga!
Hide here.

Uh-oh! We're captured.
We can't get away.

Is this **adiós** to our buckaroo day?

Off to the bunkhouse,
we make our retreat.

Hats off our heads,
and boots off our feet.

The night sky is **glowing**
with twinkly stars.

We sing with coyotes
and strum our guitars.

We're wrapped in our bedrolls
and snuggled in tight.
Buckaroo bedtime.

Buenas noches,
good night.

Glossary

Adiós *(ah-dee-**ohs**)* – Good-bye

Agua *(**ah**-gwah)* – Water

Amigo *(ah-**mee**-go)* – Friend

¡Ándale! *(**on**-da-lay)* – Hurry!

Buenas noches *(**bweh**-nahs **noh**-chayss)* – Good night

¡Caramba! *(kah-**rahm**-bah)* – Yikes!

Lobo *(**lo**-bo)* – Wolf